Awakening

Books by Lucien Stryk

Awakening

Lucien Stryk

THE SWALLOW PRESS INC.
CHICAGO

Published by
The Swallow Press Incorporated
1139 South Wabash Avenue
Chicago, Illinois 60605

ISBN (cloth) 0-8040-0332-7
ISBN (paper) 0-80-40-0333-5
LIBRARY OF CONGRESS CATALOG CARD NUMBER 73-1321-6

Acknowledgements: *Aldebaran, American Poetry Review, Ark River Review, BBC Radio 3* (London), *Carolina Quarterly, Chicago Review, December, Harvard Advocate, Hellcoal Annual, Jeopardy, Kamadhenu, Literary Review, Midwest Quarterly, The Nation, New: American and Canadian Poetry, The New Statesman, The New York Times, North American Review, Our Original Sins, Poetry Review* (London), *Rain, Road Apple Review, Saturday Review, Seneca Review, Shenandoah, Snowy Egret, Southern Poetry Review, Southwest Review, Stinktree, Strivers' Row, "Today's Poets"* (*Chicago Tribune Magazine*), *Tribune* (London), *TriQuarterly, Twentieth Century* (London), *West Coast Poetry Review, West Coast Review, Wisconsin Review.*

To Helen

always and for everything

Contents

Two: The Duckpond

The wind blows hard among the pines
Toward the beginning
Of an endless past.
Listen: you've heard everything.

—Shinkichi Takahashi

ONE:

Awakening

Awakening

Homage To Hakuin, Zen Master, 1685-1768

I

Shoichi brushed the black
on thick.
His circle held a poem
like buds
above a flowering bowl.

Since the moment of my
pointing,
this bowl, an "earth device,"
holds
nothing but the dawn.

II

A freeze last night, the window's
laced ice flowers, a meadow drifting
from the glacier's side. I think of Hakuin:

"Freezing in an icefield, stretched
thousands of miles in all directions,
I was alone, transparent, and could not move."

Legs cramped, mind pointing
like a torch, I cannot see beyond
the frost, out nor in. And do not move.

III

I balance the round stone
    in my palm,
turn it full circle,

slowly, in the late sun,
    spring to now.
Severe compression,

like a troubled head,
    stings my hand.
It falls. A small dust rises.

IV

Beyond the sycamore
dark air moves
westward—

smoke, cloud, something
wanting a name.
Across the window,

my gathered breath,
I trace
a simple word.

V

My daughter gathers shells
where thirty years before
I'd turned them over, marveling.

I take them from her,
make, at her command,
the universe. Hands clasped,

marking the limits of
a world, we watch till sundown
planets whirling in the sand.

VI

Softness everywhere,
snow a smear,
air a gray sack.

Time. Place. Thing.
Felt between
skin and bone, flesh.

VII

I write in the dark again,
rather by dusk-light,
and what I love about

this hour is the way the trees
are taken, one by one,
into the great wash of darkness.

At this hour I am always happy,
ready to be taken myself,
fully aware.

Away

Here I go again,
want to be somewhere else—
feet tramping under the desk,

I study travel brochures,
imagine monastic Hiltons,
the caravansary of my past.

Apples, cheese, a hunk of bread,
the road: what'll it be today?
I ask myself: the Seine,

Isfahan bazaar, three claps
of the hand, and Yamaguchi,
Takayama-roshi shouting—

Down, down, and breathe!
My feet go faster faster,
suddenly fly off.

Calm, breathing slowly,
I bow to Master Takayama
who smiles all the way from Japan.

Museum Guards (London)

I

He smokes against the wall
blowing rings where Moore's giants
escape through the holes

in themselves. He is small among
them, and his cigarette, the one
live thing, fizzles in the rain.

II

You would have understood what made
the guard leap from his chair
and, pointing at your saints,

cry out in Italian—
"What am I doing here?" Carlo Crivelli,
what is wrong with this world?

III

He watches us watching, weary,
cough straightening his slouch.
Seven years facing the Watteaus.

Life's no picnic. Ask him, the crippled
one who used to whisper shyly
that he was an artist, waiting for the break.

Hyde Park Sunday

Suddenly the bronzed Spaniard,
yellow bandanna on his forehead,
left his companions with a leap—
perfect somersault—then cartwheeled
past the lovers on the grass.

The sprawlers gaped, on Speakers' Corner
there was silence, those angry men
turned blessed, forgiving—
so much pure energy expended for nothing,
for absolutely nothing.

Elegy for a Long-Haired Student

He called at four a.m.: about to fly
to Mao, he had to know the Chinese word
for peace. Next day he was dead.

"Such dreams were bound for madness,"
I told his mourners. "He was too good
for this world." "He would have wanted you,"

they said. "*You* understood." Bearing
his body to the grave, I saw the long red hair
he could not stop from coiling round

their throats: Elks, Legionnaires.
Unmocked now, it would grow. As we lay
him down, I spoke that word for peace.

South

Walking at night, I always return to
       the spot beyond
the cannery and cornfields where

a farmhouse faces south among tall trees.
       I dream a life
there for myself, everything happening

in an upper room: reading in sunlight,
       talk, over wine,
with a friend, long midnight poems swept

with stars and a moon. And nothing
       being savaged,
anywhere. Having my fill of that life,

I imagine a path leading south
       through corn and wheat,
to the Gulf of Mexico! I walk

each night in practice for that walk.

Noon Report

Though yesterday, as forecast,
shot by on a wind
from the northwest,
promising nothing much,

this afternoon the blue
limbs of the sky
hang still. Up there,
as usual, something's

concocting tomorrow
which, despite the mess
we're bound to make of it,
should arrive on time.

Confession

When with my stuffed beginner's hook
    lodged in his lip
the small-mouth bass shot up
and almost ditched the rowboat, I jerked
    the flyrod high.

Caught there, eye to eye, we flashed
    together in
the sun, flyrod ablaze
between us—midspace, midlife—
    then the plunging.

I dream him down there still,
    crawdad sucked to
bone, flyrod clicking on the lakebed
where, shrunk from the anchored hulls,
    he slowly spins.

Fishing with My Daughter in Miller's Meadow

You follow, dress held high above
    the fresh manure,
missing your doll, scolding Miller's horses

for being no gentlemen where they graze
    in morning sun.
You want the river, quick, I promised you back there,

and all those fish. I point to trees where
    water rides low
banks, slopping over in the spring,

and pull you from barbed wire protecting corn
    the size of you
and gaining fast on me. To get you in the meadow

I hold the wire high, spanning a hand across
    your freckled back.
At last we make the river, skimmed with flies,

you help me scoop for bait. I give you time
    to run away,
then drop the hook. It's fish I think

I'm after, you I almost catch, in up to knees,
    sipping minnowy
water. Well, I hadn't hoped for more.

Going back, you heap the creel with phlox and marigolds.

Storm

The green horse of the tree
bucks in the wind
as lightning hits beyond.
We will ride it out together,
or together fall.

After the Storm

Slick of water on
the picnic table,
beaded lawnchairs,

street steaming in
the early heat.
Thrumming underground,

dead grass will spring
again. Half way up
the maple's trunk

the first-born squirrel's
nose. The bluejay,
like a startled eye,

darts from branch to branch.

Twister

Waiting the twister which touched down
a county north, leveled a swath
of homes, taking twenty lives,

we sit in battered chairs, southwest
corner of the basement, listen
to the radio warnings through

linoleum and creaky floorboards
of the kitchen overhead. We are
like children in a spooky film,

ghosts about to enter at the door.
I try to comfort them, though
most afraid, *Survival Handbook*

open on my lap. Around our
piled up junk cobwebs sagged with flies,
though early spring. A trunk with French Line

stickers, paint flaked in our defective
furnace heat, a stack of dishes
judged too vulgar for our guests,

sled with rusted runners, cockeyed pram
and broken dolls, Christmas trinkets
we may use again, some boards kept

mainly for the nails. I watch my wife,
son, daughter, wondering what we're up to,
what's ahead. We listen, ever

silent, for the roar out of the west,
whatever's zeroing in with terror
in its wake. The all-clear sounds,

a pop song hits above. Made it
once again. We shove the chairs
against the wall, climb into the light.

The Cherry

February: the season grips—
    heavy—the chomped
stalks in Miller's field
    across the way.

Wind comes level, spurred by
    western counties,
and horses our daughter watched
    all summer long

shiver in woodland now. Below,
    piled branches
downed by the storm of mid-December
    shift in the gusts.

We have waited a month for the city
    to cart them off—
it's been so cold the ice that
    let the storm strip

clean, has scarcely thawed. The day
    those branches split
I had to axe the cherry to its roots.
    Our girl, sulking

out of range, held tight to twigs.

Here and Now

Sunglasses upturned
on the picnic table,
where I try to write,

catch my reflection
square—sweaty, vain.
What's the use?

Hear a knocking
at the front. No muse,
a salesman

from the Alcoa
Aluminum Company
inspired by the siding

of our rented house.

Morning

I lie late where
sunlight floods the curtain,
tracing dust lines here and there.

I want to remain
floating on the sheet,
a whitecap bearing me to shores I need,

a chosen world
where no one waits
and nothing cares. Soon I shall draw

the curtain
on the window tree,
quick birds among the leaf-trace.

They build around
me, everything waits
to happen. The paper on the desk

is like a distant
sunlit pool, my pen
an indolent bather, weary of all.

Black Partridge Woods, Before a Reading

Soon words, words, words, now silence
    in the woods
of this blue-collar town.

Noon. A freight rocks rails
    lumbering
toward Chicago. Factory whistles,

everywhere, at once. Where is
    the poet
who named these woods? Mud on my shoes,

lost for an hour with the children
    of Lemont,
Illinois, I talk of partridges and poems.

Heat

Hundred degrees.
After four days
we are the sprawling
dead. The fingers

of the fan can't
claw through heat
piled up like earth.
Garbage steams

and buzzes—a page
from Dante's Hell.
Air burns the tips
of maple leaves.

Where's the rainmaker?
Somewhere black
clouds must form—
then why not here?

Summer

My neighbor frets about his lawn,
and he has reasons—
dandelions, crabgrass, a passing dog.

He scowls up at my maple, rake
clogged and trembling,
as its seeds spin down—

not angels, moths, but paratroopers
carried by the wind,
planting barricades along his eaves.

He's on the ladder now, scaring
the nibbling squirrels,
scattering starlings with his water hose.

Thank God his aim is bad
or he'd have drowned
or B-B gunned the lot. Now he

shakes a fist of seeds at me
where I sit poeming
my dandelions, crabgrass and a passing dog.

I like my neighbor, in his way
he cares for me. Look what
I've given him—something to feel superior to.

No Hitter

By the seventh it was more than a ballgame,
I crushed the rosin-bag before each pitch.

Something said: this is it, either you make
it or you don't, all life long. Either they

hit you, or you get it by them, clean.
But they were there to do the same: either they

hit me or they don't. And it would last forever.
Balanced till the bottom of the ninth, we

grimly learned the score. Whoever pitied whom,
they hit me—my no-hitter was a route.

It was relief I felt (and got)—that power
would have scared, or so I told myself.

White City

High on abandoned
rollercoaster tracks,
over Chicago,
a kite-tail in the wind,
we inched along the rotted
slats, proving ourselves
against the tug of earth.

Rivals' stones whizzing
by our ears, this was no
King-of-the-Mountain game,
we knew, as later on our knees
we worked our way below
with nothing in our hands,
not even stones.

My Daughter's Aquarium

You ask another question,
to be put off again, then
    walk away

so sad, I call you back.
It started out with birth—
    why? how? when?

From there, promised you
would hardly burst when
    that time came,

you moved on to greater perils—
beauty vanished, friends who
    always hurt.

All, things answerable, things
assurance turned to good. And
    now you're off

again, quickly from tank
to tank, passing the porpoise
    suspended

like a plastic Disney toy,
on the edge of tears,
    hating my

half answers to your questions,
blaming me as fish dart
    from your grasp.

I follow, then pull you out
into the autumn day when
    suddenly

you want to be in water,
threaten, above sobs, to
    swim away.

The Unknown Neighbor

The road you took to death
I traveled on, three hours before,
and made it safely home.

I hadn't met you, being me,
but often saw you home
from work, circled by kids

shrieking as you tossed
them up, again, again,
your wife tall in the doorway,

almost too tired to smile.
You were the perfect neighbor—
lawn mowing, leaf raking,

unborrowing—just so for
our town. And now your door
is shut, your family gone

five months since your death
to another husband, father.
Leaves pile high on lawn

and sidewalk, still throughout
the neighborhood fly rumors
of a widow's nights.

TWO:

The Duckpond

The Duckpond

I

Crocus, daffodil:
    already the pond's
        clear of ice

where, winter long,
    ducks and gulls
        slid for crusts.

People circle—
    pale, bronchitic,
        jostling behind dogs,

grope toward lawnchairs
    spread like islands
        on the grass.

Sunk there, they lift faces to the sun.

II

Good Friday.
    Ducks carry on,
        a day like any other.

Same old story:
    no one seems to care.
        A loudmouth

leader of a mangy host
    spiked to a cross,
        as blackbirds in certain

lands neighboring on
    that history are splayed
        on fences, warning

to their kind. A duck soars from the reeds.

III

Man and woman
   argue past the duckpond,
         his arms flaying,

she, head down—even
   by the fully budded
         cherry, clustered

lilac boughs. Not once
   do they forget
         their bitterness,

face the gift of morning
   ducks wake to
         in the reeds.

They have things to settle, and they will.

IV

On my favorite
 bench beside the roses
  I watch ducks

smoothing feathers,
 breathing it all in.
  Catching the headline

where the bird flits
 I'm reminded
  three men were shot up

at the moon. I turn
 back to the roses:
  what

if they don't make it? If they do?

V

Lying near the pond
 in fear of the stray
  dog that daily

roams the park,
 ducks know
  their limitations,

and the world's—
 how long it takes,
  precisely,

to escape the paw thrusts
 of the dog,
  who once again

swings round to chase his tail.

VI

Radio tower
    beyond the blossoms,
        ducks

here in the pond,
    a connection
        between them—

how did I discover
    this, and why?
        Was it

the blue air? The bench
    moves beneath
        us like a seesaw,

the pond sends news of the world.

VII

What becomes of things
    we make or do?
        The Japanese lantern

or from across the pond
    beneath the trees
        a drift

of voices cultured
    and remote: water
        will carry anything

that floats. The lantern
    maker, the couple
        chatting there

would be amazed to find themselves a poem.

VIII

When tail wagging
    in the breeze
        the duck pokes

bill into the pondbed,
    keeps it there,
        my daughter thinks

him fun—he is, yet how to say
    those acrobatics
        aren't meant

to jollify the day. He's
    hungry, poking
        away at nothing

for crumbs we failed to bring: how to tell her?

IX

Ducks lie close together
    in morning dew, wary eyed,
        bills pointing at the pond:

roused by squirrels,
    those early risers,
        air's a-whir with wings.

Sad to think of leaving
    this place. A helicopter
        with mysterious purpose

appears above the trees,
    moving low. Its circles
        tightening,

the ducks cling to the pondedge, right to fear.

The Edge

Living that year at the edge
of the ravine,
sloped down to the woods, we listened

to the animals before the town
awoke, blurring
the limits of our days,

forcing its round, the needs
of others.
Near sleep, after loving, we felt

part of a stillness with the dark
and all its creatures,
holding to the edge of where we lived.

For Helen

You chip a tooth, complain
of getting old.
Well, I've felt old for years.

"You're as old
as you are,"
I quip and parry frowns.

"Look, we're in this
together"—that
never fails, you're in

my arms and young. Warmth
to warmth, we're
bound to last forever.

Map

I unfold it on the desk
to trace you once again.
Though cut off by a smudge

of mountains, ropes
of water stretched between,
how easily I spread a hand

across the space that separates.
　　　　　　But this
cramped sheet, while true,

does not tell all. What of
that span no map will ever
show, sharper for being unseen?

The Writer's Wife

Deep in your northwood's fastness,
snowbound half the year, you complain,

he tells me, of problems with the stove,
dirt, loneliness, yet says he's proud

of your tenacity, your faith in him.
Meanwhile he writes what only you will read.

No one else would do this for him,
he whose work has come to nothing.

Amputee

Something kept the blood from
going round—
he gave up one leg like a prize,

and then the other. Soon it would
be his arms.
He called it an "unwilling heart."

Jollying nurses, once he rocked
the ward with—
"Who's for football?" from his bedpan throne.

When he was readied for the saw again,
we wished him
well. He waved his bandaged hand:

"Now you see it, now you don't,"
he quipped. They
told us he died laughing under gas.

Boston

South Station, very early, and
come to read midwestern poems
at Tufts, due in an hour, seedy

in my all-night-slept-in suit,
I need a shave. The john of Savarin's
is full. I try the public one.

A bum is scraping skin off
at the mirror. I stand behind him,
fumble for the switch, lift

my cordless shaver to the jaw.
The tatooed stripper on his arm
begins to bump. Soap drips bloody

from his straightedge. "Give it here,"
he mutters. Razor plowing down,
I know he means it, hand

it to him, juice full on,
grab my suitcase, then half shaved
move off to read those poems.

The Exchange

As I turned from the bar,
my back to him,
he beat it through the door
with every cent I had.

"Happens everyday," the barkeep
said. I burned for weeks,
imagined trapping him
in alleyways, fists ready.

Then his face lost focus,
I found myself remembering
the tip he gave me
on a horse, his winning manner

and his guts. I'd learned
at some expense
a truth about myself,
and was twice robbed.

The Loser

He's there outside again, holding up
the tavern wall, whatever the day.

Never completely under—cadging,
wheedling through his tale. Few seem

to pity him. Others remember the girl
who ditched him for a carnival,

and promised she'd be back. So his
long wait began. Well, someone had to hurt,

and he was chosen: town drunk, town loser,
plastered with the ads against the wall.

Clown

Brush in hand, blinking
    under
        a sombrero of whitewash,

he's shoved feetfirst
    into
        the cannon's mouth.

Drums pointing in their chests
    children
        hold their ears.

It's no surprise to them
    that,
        blast still ringing,

he hits the net and springs up
    bloodless,
        on his toes.

The Last Romantic

"Le Duc" we hailed him to his pinched
Napoleonic face, behind
the frail brushed back, "Le Fou."

All day he'd prowl the boulevards,
gilt cane ticking, for Insult,
and when he found it, up went cane

and swish! another passer-by'd
be sliced and stacked like sausage
on the dark shelf of his mind.

Thus Le Duc until that chilly
afternoon at Jean's Café.
There he perched, like a hawk, for

Slight. The tourist hardly stopped
to gawk inside: more than enough.
"Crapaud!" Le Duc arose and charged—

what a shattering of pride!
Before they shrove him of Jean's
windowglass, Le poor Fou died.

To Roger Blin

My shaky French, my coarse
Bohemian ways,
must have amused you—

you who had the "mark,"
the fiery
haunted look of postwar Paris.

Sweating over poems
in a drab
leftbank hotel, I fantasized

your life, slowly to feel
as you directed
Lorca's plays, myself

upon that stage. Was it
a style, warm
and yet severe, an honesty?

Now opening Genet's *Letters
to Roger Blin,*
I feel ashamed. I asked

too much of you: a path,
a way, the art
to make life possible.

Dean Dixon, Welcome Home

Weary of their praise—"those
black expressive hands,"
tired of saying Brahms

not Gershwin was your man,
you left behind do-gooders
and their scented wives,

sailed from their "Negro Firsts"
to prove you had the gift.
Now, tall before the orchestra,

drawing urgent chords, you raise
those hands again. Times
are changed, they say, and someone

needs what you alone can give.
Seasons late, you're
welcomed home, Dean Dixon, friend.

Busker

Facing the playhouse queue,
straining through songs

all can remember, she muffs
a high note at the end.

As we start to shuffle in,
she scrambles for the loot.

Fat, seedy—never mind—
she is so purely what she is

no actor could do more.
Leaving the queue, I follow

her all night, hands full of coins,
songs ringing everywhere.

Church Concert (London)

Juan Arrau, guitarist, your Frescobaldi,
      Albeniz,
stir the crowded aisles of Saint Martin's,

warm the shivering woman, feet tapping
      on the pew,
and the man dozing against a pillar looks

wildly where the stained glass shatters in
      the priest's eyes.
You pierce them with a deep song from your

native South—the rush of sea, waves like
      horns against
a wall. The audience set free, Trafalgar Square

will never be the same—Nelson like
      a prowhead,
adrift once more upon the Spanish Main.

Keats House

I sign the guest book
where some wit scrawled—
"Keats had a sore Fanny!"

Move by books, portraits,
manuscripts, his chair.
Sad—I get the feel of him,

yet something's gone,
whatever made him write:
the girl, a nightingale,

seasons of mist, which had
their music too? Beyond
the house the Heath's

not as it was, yet cold enough
to raise that chill which
kept him in these rooms, a poet

and a dying man, to do the work.

At Shakespeare's Tomb

Tickets trailing from their fists, whispering
    about the need
    to patch, renew,
the priests take our money, lead us where

you lie boxed in beneath your likeness.
    Outside the Avon
    active with
detergent, crested here and there by dizzy swans.

Along the banks your worshippers vision you
    wading, fishing,
    rushing past them
with a mate, poached deer on shouldered pole.

Naughty, you charm them, as in the playhouse
    down the river
    you'll amaze.
In spite of Lear you have become an industry:

ten fleets of bus, fifteen Chinese cooks,
    five Italian,
    a pox of
Ye Olde this and that, guides in your father's

and your daughter's houses—possibly
    your trundle bed,
    likely your
chamberpot. Tourists, cameras weighing

down their heads, seize you at last. Meanwhile
    a grateful bed-
    and-breakfast town
rejoices in your power, its poetry.

Sniper

An inch to the left
and I'd be twenty years
of dust by now. I can't

walk under trees without
his muzzle tracks me.
He'd hit through branches,

leaves pinned to his shoulders
whistling. We searched him
everywhere—up trunks,

in caves, down pits. Then
one night, his island taken,
he stepped from jungle

shade, leaves still pinned
upon him glistening
in the projector's light,

and tiptoed round to watch
our show, a weary kid
strayed in from trick-or-treat.

Forward Observers

Our lensed hill-splitting eyes
useless in the dark, they
flanked us through the night.

Indispensable, we called
down thunder from the hills,
and saved a thousand.

Each of us worth, some claimed,
one hundred men,
they needed yet despised us.

Their bodies held like sandbags.
We survived,
part of something coming, vile as war.

Thoroughbred Country

Lexington to Louisville: the Greyhound
moves through bluegrass, the stud, its mares,
caught delicately on the soft hill.

It's all horse talk past Calumet,
"richest acres" in the world.
Blue—the grass, the sky, the blood.

Conscripts in the bus, straight
from the hollows, first time away,
are wondering what awaits them.

A black horse gallops from the shadows.
The young men look away.
No one speaks until we enter Louisville.

Evening

Weary, I seek relief behind
the paper, before the set
where they emerge, the victims,

through walls and floorboards,
summoning to a ritual
hung with fear, myself enacted,

inflicting and inflicted pain.
From fissures in the earth,
from smoking thatch they rush

toward me, arms like torches,
children grasped between,
cries hurtling oceans meant

to separate. What can I do?
Put down, switch off—
plunge to the barricades of sleep.

Sunday. The Bells.

All over town they
rise from beds,
heavy with dreams
of sons dying in Viet Nam.

Sunday. The bells ring
in the terrible emptiness
of bedrooms their distant
sons dream girls into.

Letter to Jean-Paul Baudot, at Christmas

Friend, on this sunny day, snow sparkling
everywhere, I think of you once more,
how many years ago, a child Resistance

fighter trapped by Nazis in a cave
with fifteen others, left to die, you became
a cannibal. Saved by Americans,

the taste of a dead comrade's flesh foul
in your mouth, you fell onto the snow
of the Haute Savoie and gorged to purge yourself,

somehow to start again. Each winter since
you were reminded, vomiting for days.
Each winter since you told me at the Mabillon,

I see you on the first snow of the year
spreadeagled, face buried in that stench.
I write once more, Jean-Paul, though you don't

answer, because I must: today men do far worse.
Yours in hope of peace, for all of us,
before the coming of another snow.